Margret Rey

Pretzel

With Pictures by H. A. Rey

Harper & Row, Publishers

One morning in May
five little dachshunds were born.

One of them was Pretzel.

They grew up the way puppies do and they all looked exactly alike the first few weeks.

Paul

Patricia

Priscilla

Percival

But after nine weeks Pretzel suddenly started growing—and growing—and growing.

**He grew much longer
than any of his brothers and sisters.**

And when he was fully grown he had become
the longest dachshund in all the world.

Pretzel was pleased with himself because it is very distinguished for a dachshund to be so long.

When he was one year old (a dachshund is grown up at that age) he won the Blue Ribbon at the Dog Show which means that everybody considered him the best looking dog of all.

All the dogs admired him.
And all the people admired him.

Only Greta didn't.

Greta was
the little dachshund
from across the street.
Pretzel was in love with her
and wanted to marry her.

But Greta just laughed at him.
"I don't care for long dogs," she said.
"But it is very distinguished for a dachshund
to be so long and I won the
Blue Ribbon at the Dog Show," said Pretzel.
"I still don't care," said Greta.
Pretzel was hurt but he did not show it.
"Please marry me," he said, "and I will
do anything for you!"
"Prove it!" said Greta and went away.

So Pretzel set out to prove it.
First he brought Greta a nice big bone.
"Thanks for the bone," said Greta,
"But I won't marry you for that.
I don't care for long dogs."
And she ate the bone and forgot about Pretzel.

Pretzel had to try something else.
He gave her the lovely green rubber ball
he had been given for his birthday.

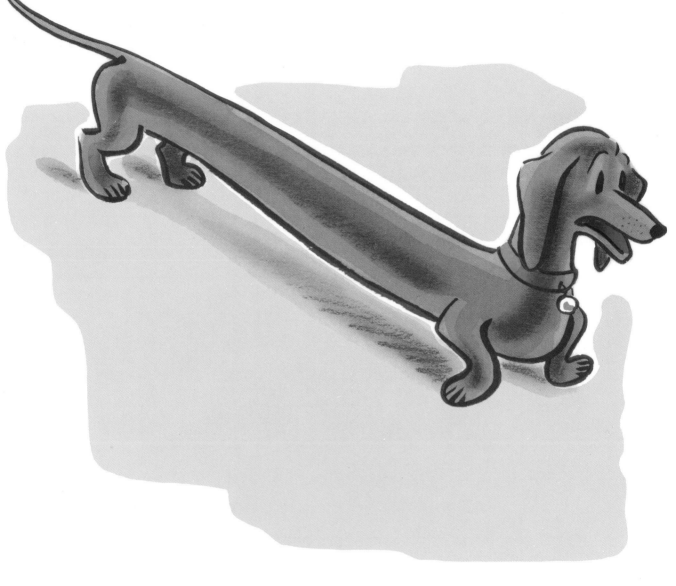

"Thank you," said Greta,
"but I still won't marry you
because I don't care for long dogs.
Besides, everybody can give *presents!*"
And she ran away with the ball.

"Look what I can do!
Nobody except me can do THAT!"
said Pretzel when they met again.

And this is what he did:

"Not bad," said Greta. "Your name certainly fits you. But I like the pretzels at the baker's better, and I still don't care for long dogs." Pretzel was very unhappy.

Some weeks had passed and Greta hadn't even spoken to Pretzel. One day while she was playing with her green ball it bounced away. Greta tried to catch it and boomps! they both landed in a hole.

Greta tried to get out of the hole, but she couldn't. It was much too deep. She was terribly scared. If nobody came to save her she might never, never...Just then Pretzel's face appeared over the edge of the hole.

"I'll get you out of there!" he shouted.
(He had watched Greta all the time

and now had rushed to help her.)
How good that Pretzel was so long!

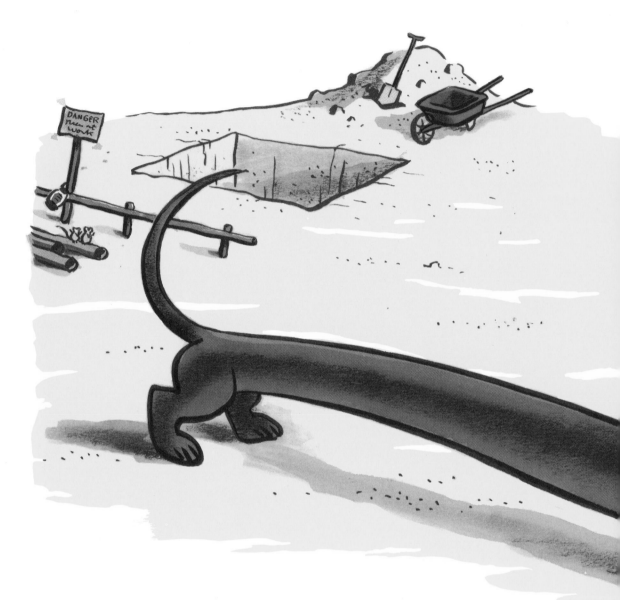

"I believe you saved my life. You are wonderful!" said Greta with a sigh.
"Will you marry me now?" asked Pretzel.

"I will," said Greta,
"but not for your length!"
So they kissed each other,

and got married,

and one morning in May
five little dachshunds were born...